In memory of my father, Garrett Bowers Hutts, and to Eri,
who loves airplanes and orca whales—D. H. A.

To choopmonkey, Anne-Marie—K. M.

LOONY LITTLE

THE ICE CAP IS MELTING!

Dianna Hutts Aston

Illustrated by Kelly Murphy

Charlesbridge

On a cold summer night, when the Arctic sun was shining brightly, a drop of water fell—plop!—on Loony Little's head.

"GREAT TOP OF THE WORLD!"
she wailed. "The polar ice cap is melting!
I must go tell the Polar Bear Queen!"

PLOP!

Loony Little flew northward as fast as she could. On a high cliff she met Dovekie Lovekie.

"Where are you going, Loony Little?" asked Dovekie Lovekie.

"The polar ice cap is melting, and I am going to tell the Polar Bear Queen," replied Loony Little.

"GOODNESS GLACIERS!" squawked Dovekie Lovekie. "Why is it melting? I will come with you and ask the Polar Bear Queen."

The two flew on northward until they spied
Puffin Muffin floating on the sea.
"Where are you going?" asked Puffin Muffin.
"The polar ice cap is melting, and we are going
to tell the Polar Bear Queen," replied Loony Little
and Dovekie Lovekie.

"SUFFERING PUFFALUMPS!"

screeched Puffin Muffin. "Without ice, we can't live! I will come with you to tell the Polar Bear Queen."

The three swam along until they met Harey
Clarey on the shore.

"Where are you going?" asked Harey Clarey.

"The polar ice cap is melting, and we are going
to tell the Polar Bear Queen," replied Loony
Little, Dovekie Lovekie, and Puffin Muffin.

"LEAPING LEMMINGS!" snuffled Harey Clarey. "If the ice cap melts, the sea will rise, and my den might flood! I will come with you and tell the Polar Bear Queen."

So they scooted and waddled and hopped
northward until they met Sealy Sally
coming up for a breath of air.

"Where are you going?" asked Sealy Sally.
"The polar ice cap is melting, and we are going
to tell the Polar Bear Queen," replied Loony Little,
Dovekie Lovekie, Puffin Muffin, and Harey Clarey.

"BE CAREFUL!"
barked Sealy Sally.
"The Polar Bear Queen
ate my cousin just last week—
she will eat all of you, too!"

Sealy Sally slipped back into the sea.

"OH, DEAR!"
wailed
Loony Little.

"OH, MY!"
squawked
Dovekie Lovekie.

"OH, NO!"
screeched
Puffin Muffin.

"LET'S NOT TELL THE POLAR BEAR QUEEN,"
snuffled Harey Clarey.

Just then Foxy Loxy appeared. "Where are you going in such a rush?" he asked.

"We *were* going to see the Polar Bear Queen," said Loony Little.

"To tell her the ice cap is melting," said Dovekie Lovekie.

"But Sealy Sally told us the Polar Bear Queen is dangerous," said Puffin Muffin.

"So we are turning back," said Harey Clarey.

"Oh no, *please* don't turn back," said Foxy Loxy. "Not without delivering such *important* news."

"BUT THE POLAR BEAR QUEEN MIGHT EAT US!" wailed Loony Little.

"No, she won't," said Foxy Loxy. "Not if I escort you. Come, I will take you to her."

And so Loony Little, Dovekie Lovekie, Puffin Muffin, and Harey Clarey followed Foxy Loxy. But Loony Little, who couldn't waddle or hop as well as the others, fell behind.

"WAIT FOR ME!"

cried Loony Little, tripping over something in the snow.

"STOP!"

Loony Little wailed. "We've been tricked!
That's Foxy Loxy's lair—he's going to eat us!"
Thinking quickly, she pecked a nugget of ice
from the ground and flung it at Foxy Loxy.
It hit him squarely on the head.

"GREAT MIDNIGHT SUN!"

howled Foxy Loxy. "The polar ice cap *is* melting!
I must go tell the Polar Bear Queen!"
In a blur of fur, he took off running.

Foxy Loxy found the Polar Bear Queen sprawled near a hole in the ice, waiting for Sealy Sally to come up for air.

"QUICK, RUN FOR YOUR LIFE!" shouted Foxy Loxy. "The polar ice cap is melting!"

"HOW AWFUL!"

roared the Polar Bear Queen. "Tell me
more—after dinner."

And she *ate* Foxy Loxy.

Soon the four friends were safe on a southerly course.

"Oh, my GOODNESS! The Polar Bear
Queen *is* dangerous!" said Dovekie Lovekie.

"And she DOESN'T SEEM TO CARE
about the ice cap melting," said Puffin Muffin.

"There must be SOMETHING we can do," said Loony Little.

"What SHOULD we do?" asked Harey Clarey.

"It's up to us to find out," Loony Little replied.

"ALL OF US."

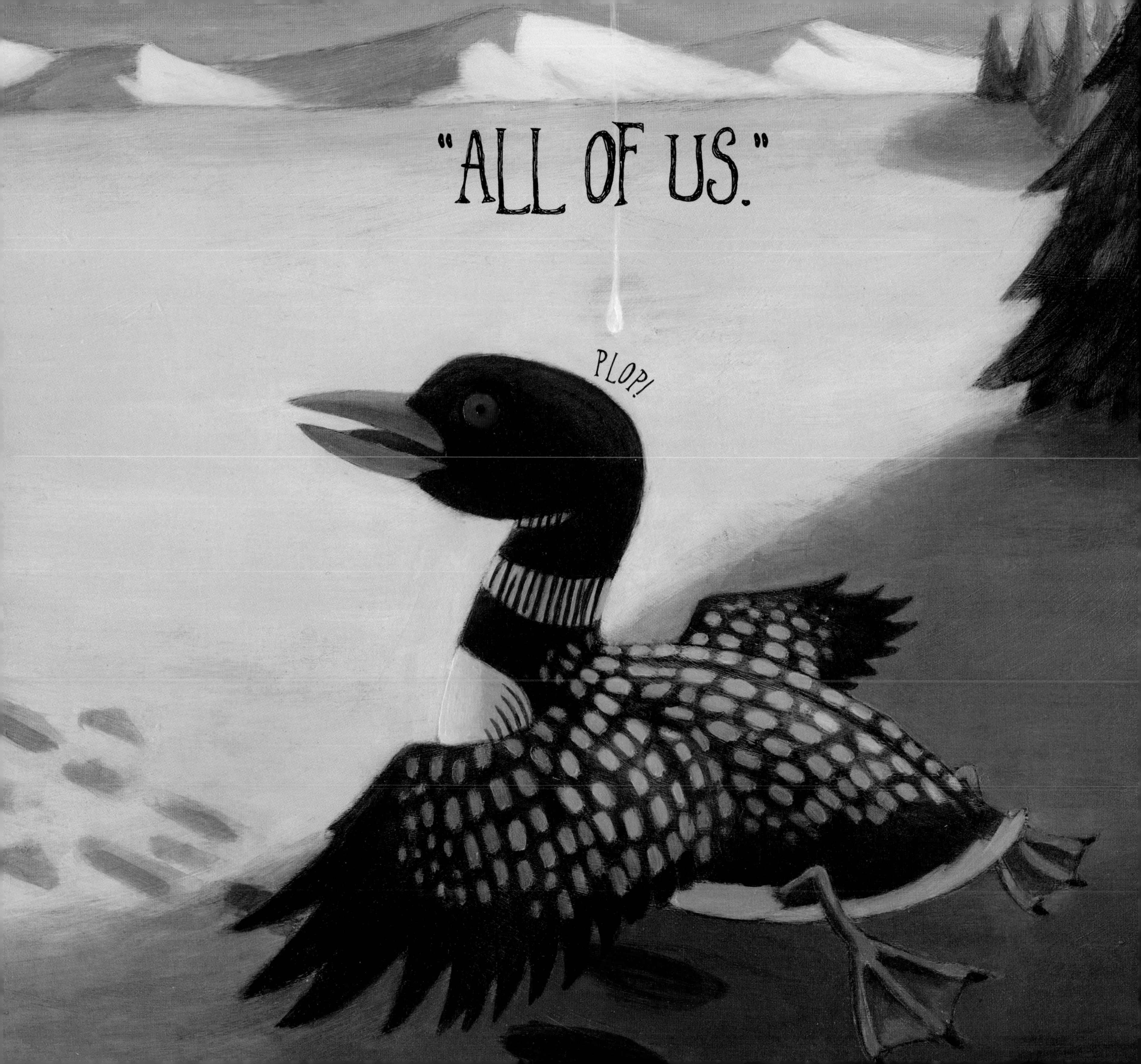

AUTHOR'S NOTE

Today most scientists agree that human activities have led to climate changes from the North Pole, where these Arctic creatures live, to the South Pole, where other animals live. Here are some effects of the climate crisis:

- Higher temperatures on Earth's surface.
- Sea ice thinning and glaciers melting. (Polar animals need the ice because they live on it.)
- More extreme weather, such as hurricanes, tornadoes, and heat and cold waves; and occurrences such as earthquakes and volcanic eruptions.
- Increases and decreases in rainfall that produce floods and droughts.

HOW EARTH TAKES IN HEAT

Think of Earth as a greenhouse. Sunlight shines year-round, keeping the plants warm. Plants and trees "inhale" gases such as carbon dioxide and "exhale" oxygen. As the sun warms the Earth, these natural gases control the climate the way a greenhouse does. They trap some heat and release some into space. This is called "the greenhouse effect." Without the natural greenhouse effect, our planet would be too cold for most life. But if human activities change this natural cycle and extra carbon dioxide is produced, Earth traps more heat. It gets too warm. This is called global warming.

There are human activities that release unhealthy amounts of carbon dioxide into the atmosphere:

- The use of fossil fuels, such as oil, gas, and coal, that power factories, cars, planes, tractors, lawn mowers, and more.
- Deforestation, or cutting down and burning trees to create more farmland, roads, parking lots, and buildings. Most deforestation occurs in tropical rain forests.
- Using batteries that charge our cell phones, computers, and other gadgets.

Other greenhouse gases created by human activities are methane and nitrous oxide. Raising livestock—like cows, pigs, chickens, and sheep—in large numbers, such as on feedlots, releases these gases through animal waste.

What will happen if people continue to use fuels that make Earth's temperature rise? What will happen if we do not find other sources of energy to charge our electronics? Will rising sea levels wash away coastal cities and farmland? Will plants and people and other animals suffer even more extreme weather?

What questions do you have? As Loony Little says at the end of the story, you can try to find out what to do. Discovering ways to make the Earth healthier requires all of us to learn and to take action.

WHAT YOU CAN DO

- Ask adults how the weather has changed since they were children.

- Talk to experts about other energy sources we can use besides fossil fuels. Invite a local TV meteorologist to visit your school.

- Brainstorm the "ripple effects" of climate change. For instance, extremely cold temperatures can cause water pipes to burst. If that happens, it could be more difficult for firefighters to put out fires.

- Organize a tree-planting day—trees provide oxygen.

- Turn off the lights when you leave a room. Saving electricity saves energy.

- Walk or ride your bike to school instead of taking the bus. Reduce your "carbon footprint."

- Grow a vegetable garden. Eating locally saves the energy it takes to transport food.

- Create a science book club. What else can you learn?

- Conduct simple experiments. For example, to find out what happens when the ice cap melts, place miniature animals (or other small items) on an icy surface such as a cake pan of frozen water. Take it out of the freezer and let it warm up. What happens when the ice begins to melt? Does the water level rise? What happens to the animals?

TAKE ACTION!

ABOUT THE ANIMALS

COMMON LOON

The common loon has a call that can sound like a wail, a laugh, or even a yodel. The loon is a skilled swimmer, diver, and flier—however, because its webbed feet are close to its tail, it scoots on land by pushing itself along on its chest. Loons are thriving and are not endangered.

DOVEKIE

These small birds are a favorite prey of Arctic foxes. During the summer, when the sun shines even at midnight, millions of dovekies swarm toward their nesting grounds, forming fluttering black ribbons that can stretch for miles above the waves. Populations are decreasing somewhat, but most scientists think there's not a cause for concern of extinction.

ATLANTIC PUFFIN

A short-necked bird that spends most of its time near the sea, the puffin returns to land only to nest. Its beak becomes bright orange and yellow during mating season. Puffins can live to be twenty years old. This bird is listed as vulnerable, and some organizations consider it threatened with extinction.

ARCTIC HARE

Arctic hares of the far north keep their white coats year-round. Their wide hind paws act as snowshoes so that hares can move quickly across the snow. The Arctic hare can hop on two legs, like a kangaroo does. The hare population is doing well.

SEAL

There are many species of seals in the Arctic. A seal can hold its breath underwater for twenty minutes or more. When the seas freeze over in winter, seals make breathing holes in the ice. Polar bears often catch seals at or near the surface of their breathing holes. Most Arctic seal species have healthy numbers and are not endangered.

ARCTIC FOX

An adult Arctic fox weighs about as much as a house cat, but its bushy coat—white in winter, brownish gray in summer—makes it look much larger. Foxes follow polar bears and feed on their leftovers. They also eat small mammals, birds, and bird eggs. This species is not endangered, but they are still poached by humans in some parts of the world for their beautiful coats.

POLAR BEAR

The largest, most powerful hunter in the Arctic, the polar bear wanders the polar ice to hunt seal, its favorite food. With its webbed front paws, the polar bear is an excellent swimmer and can swim many miles in search of food. Polar bears are vulnerable because the melting ice is where they live. There are many conservation efforts under way to save them, and you can search online for more information.

MORE INFORMATION

MOTHER EARTH NEWS

https://www.motherearthnews.com
This magazine includes information about organic foods, country living, green transportation, renewable energy, natural health, and green building. Search for articles about fossil fuels.

NASA CLIMATE KIDS

https://climatekids.nasa.gov/greenhouse-effect/
This website has information about Earth's climate just for kids!

NATIONAL CLIMATE ASSESSMENT

https://nca2014.globalchange.gov
This organization summarizes how climate change affects the United States.

NATIONAL OCEANIC AND ATMOSPHERIC ADMINISTRATION

https://www.noaa.gov/resource-collections/climate-change-impacts
NOAA's scientists provide citizens, emergency managers, and others with important information.

NATIONAL SNOW AND ICE DATA CENTER

https://nsidc.org
They work to increase knowledge about Earth's frozen regions.

POLAR SCIENCE CENTER

http://psc.apl.uw.edu
They research the ice-covered regions on Earth.

Text copyright © 2020 by Dianna Hutts Aston
Illustrations copyright © 2003 by Kelly Murphy

Published by Charlesbridge
85 Main Street, Watertown, MA 02472
(617) 926-0329 • www.charlesbridge.com

Library of Congress Cataloging-in-Publication Data
Names: Aston, Dianna Hutts, author. | Murphy, Kelly, 1977– illustrator.
Title: Loony Little : the ice cap is melting / Dianna Hutts Aston ;
    illustrated by Kelly Murphy.
Description: Watertown, MA : Charlesbridge, [2020] | Originally published in
    a slightly different form in Cambridge, Massachusetts, by Candlewick in
    2003. | Summary: In this adaptation of the Chicken Little story, Loony
    Little, worried that the polar ice cap is melting, sets out to tell the
    Polar Bear Queen, gathering animal friends as she goes—but, as Sealy
    Sally warns them, the Polar Bear Queen is more interested in making a
    lunch of Loony Little and her friends. | Includes bibliographical
    references.
Identifiers: LCCN 2018058510 (print) | LCCN 2019001919 (ebook) |
    ISBN 9781632898869 (ebook) | ISBN 9781632898876 (ebook pdf) |
    ISBN 9781623541170 (reinforced for library use)
Subjects: LCSH: Chicken Licken—Adaptations—Juvenile fiction. |
    Birds—Juvenile fiction. | Polar bear—Juvenile fiction. |
    Animals—Juvenile fiction. | Climatic changes—Juvenile fiction. | Global
    warming—Juvenile fiction. | Arctic regions—Juvenile fiction. | CYAC:
    Animals—Arctic regions—Fiction. | Climatic changes—Fiction. | Global
    warming—Fiction. | Arctic regions—Fiction.
Classification: LCC PZ7.A8483 (ebook) | LCC PZ7.A8483 Lo 2020 (print) |
    DDC 813.6 [E]—dc23
LC record available at https://lccn.loc.gov/2018058510

Printed in China
(hc) 10 9 8 7 6 5 4 3 2 1

Illustrations done in acrylic, watercolor, and gel medium on board
Display type set in Lovers Avenue by Creativeqube
Text type set in Jacoby by Image Club Graphics, Inc.
Color separations by Colourscan Print Co Pte Ltd, Singapore
Printed by 1010 Printing International Limited in Huizhou, Guangdong, China
Production supervision by Brian G. Walker
Designed by Jacqueline Noelle Cote